On Christmas Eve

On Christmas Eve

by Ann M. Martin

Illustrations by Jon J Muth

SCHOLASTIC INC.

NEW YORK TORONTO LONDON AUCKLAND SYDNEY
MEXICO CITY NEW DELHI HONG KONG BUENOS AIRES

No part of this publication may be reproduced, stored in a retrieval system, or transmitted in any form or by any means, electronic, mechanical, photocopying, recording, or otherwise, without written permission of the publisher. For information regarding permission, write to Scholastic Inc., Attention: Permissions Department, 557 Broadway, New York, NY 10012.

This book was originally published in hardcover by Scholastic Press in 2006.

ISBN-13: 978-0-439-74589-5
ISBN-10: 0-439-74589-6

12 11 10 9 8 7 6 5 4 3   8 9 10 11 12/0

Printed in the U.S.A.   40
First Scholastic paperback printing, October 2007

For my father,

who showed me the

magic of Christmas

*I*t was Christmas Eve of 1958 when I saw Santa Claus, the real Santa Claus.

That was last year, when I was eight. Now I am nine, and it is December 24th again, and I am lying in bed, waiting. I open the window so that I can feel the crackling Christmas Eve air. I watch as the light from the big star above the trees beyond the Andersons' barn shines brighter and brighter. And I jump when I hear a noise in the hallway.

"Tess? Are you awake?" Evvie pokes her head into my room.

I let out my breath and tell my heart to stop beating so fast. "I'm awake," I reply.

My sister dashes barefoot across the floor and leaps onto the bed.

"I can't sleep," she says, and I know why. Evvie is twelve

years old, and she has asked our parents for a makeup kit for Christmas. She is beside herself with excitement over the idea of being able to wear lipstick and maybe some blue eye shadow in order to impress Wesley Johnson, who is a year ahead of Evvie at Hopewell Junior High. Our parents would have a fit if they knew that's why Evvie wants this present, which I don't think they have bought for her anyway.

"I can't sleep either," I tell Evvie.

We are excited, but for very different reasons. I don't say anything about this to Evvie, though. Evvie does not believe in Santa or in the magical world that is part of our every-day world — the one that is there sort of at the edges, something you might be able to see out of the corner of your eye if you turn to just the right place at just the right moment.

If you truly believe.

One

The autumn of 1958 blows in on a wild and chilly wind. People in Hopewell say they can't remember an October like it. By the beginning of November, Evvie and I have to bundle up in scarves and mittens and woolen hats, and then in our galoshes as the snow starts to fly.

Each weekday morning we stand at the end of our lane and wait for the bus. Evvie still goes to my school this year. I am in third grade and Evvie is in sixth. While we wait, we stamp our feet and rub our mittened hands together. Sometimes during this autumn that feels more like a winter, our mother even sends us off to Hopewell Elementary wearing ski pants under our dresses, but we have to take them off when we get to school because of the "no pants for girls" rule.

"We're going to have a white Christmas for sure this year," Dad keeps saying.

I am thrilled. The snow is part of the excitement of an autumn that has left me nearly breathless.

It is on a Saturday early in December when I decide that I am going to see Santa for myself — the real one, not a department store Santa in a faded suit with a limp beard. And I am going to see him in our own living room during the time of enchantment that I am sure begins at midnight on Christmas Eve. Midnight is a powerful hour on an ordinary night, but on

Christmas Eve it's the start of an especially magical time.

I wake up early that Saturday, long before Evvie, who could sleep for hours and hours on weekend mornings.

In the kitchen I find Dad standing at the stove stirring a pot of oatmeal. Mom is hanging up the phone, brows knitted, eyes serious.

"Good morning," I say as I slide into my seat at the table.

"Morning, pumpkin," says Dad.

"Morning," says Mom. "Tess, that was Mrs. Benjamin. Sarah's going to spend the weekend with us again."

Something tightens in my stomach. Now I know why Mom looks worried. "I thought Mr. Benjamin was going to come home," I say.

Mom shakes her head. "Maybe next week."

"So he'll be home for Christmas."

"I hope so," Mom replies.

The grown-ups have promised that Mr. Benjamin will be home for Christmas. Promised. He has to come home. Christmas is not a time for things to go wrong.

Sarah is my best friend. Her mother is Mom's best friend. Mrs. Benjamin and Mom met when they were in the hospital giving birth to Sarah and me. (I am two hours older than Sarah.)

Sarah and I have grown up together. I have spent more time with Sarah than with Evvie. (Sarah doesn't have any brothers or sisters.) Sometimes Sarah and I pretend we are twin sisters, even though we look nothing alike. We have sleepovers all the time, and our own private club called Twins Not Twins, and we were in the same class in nursery school and first grade, and now in third grade. In kindergarten we had the same teacher, but I was in morning kindergarten, and Sarah was in afternoon kindergarten, and it was horrible because that was also the first year I had to ride the bus, and the only person I knew on our route was Evvie, who wouldn't let me sit with her, except on the first day of school. After that I was on my own.

The Benjamins live three miles away, but Sarah and I see each other almost every day, even when we are not in school. The bottom bunk in Sarah's room is called Tess's bed. Last summer I went to the mountains with the Benjamins, and Sarah went to the beach with my family.

Then, in October, when the chilly wind was starting to screech around the houses and barns of Hopewell, Mr. Benjamin said he didn't feel well. He went to the doctor. He went to the hospital. And the grown-ups began to talk of cancer. They always said the word in a whisper. "He has . . . *cancer*."

The more time Mr. Benjamin spends in the hospital, the more time Sarah spends with us. Sometimes she is here for whole weeks. (It is so unfair that kids aren't allowed to visit people in the hospital, not even when those people are their own parents.) Mr.

Benjamin was supposed to come home from the hospital yesterday. Sarah even strung together eleven sheets of construction paper to make a sign that reads WELCOME HOME, one big letter on each piece of paper. She said she was going to hang it over the front door to surprise her father.

"Why didn't Mr. Benjamin come home?" I ask Mom.

Mom shakes her head. She doesn't know. Nobody seems to know much about the *cancer*. "Sarah will be here by lunchtime," says Mom.

And this is when I decide that I must see the real Santa. I have to talk to him. It's very important.

I am poking at the oatmeal Dad spooned into my bowl when I think I feel someone staring at me. I peek under the table and there is Sadie. She is sitting at my feet, looking up at me with her happy squinty eyes.

I consider Sadie my second best friend. Which frankly dumbfounds Evvie.

"A dog can't be your best friend," she has said many times.

I don't see why not. Sadie and I spend as much time together as Sarah and I do. And I talk to Sadie, tell her all sorts of things. Especially things Sarah doesn't want to talk about, like her father's illness.

Sadie always looks at me when I talk to her and cocks her head, and if I tell her something particularly interesting, she lifts her ears as if she understands me. Which is what a best friend is all about. I wish Sadie could answer me, but I guess that isn't possible. If it were, Sadie surely would have spoken by now.

I found Sadie in the ditch by our road when she was a puppy. We took her to our vet, Dr. Leighton, and he guessed at her age. "About sixteen weeks, I'd say, judging by her teeth." Now Sadie is three years old. She looks like a miniature golden retriever with a cocker spaniel head and a terrier body.

"She's a mutt," Evvie says, but Evvie loves her too.

I finish my breakfast and leave Mom and Dad reading the paper at the kitchen table. Evvie is still asleep. I want her to wake up. I am hoping Maggie, who is Evvie's best friend, will come over today so Sarah and I can watch her and Evvie do eleven-year-old things. Sarah always says this helps her forget about the hospital. We will try not to be pests.

I know better than to wake up Evvie, though, so I decide to take Sadie for a walk.

"Bundle up," Mom calls from the kitchen.

The snow is flying again.

I bundle up until I feel like a pillow stuffed into its case. Then I call to Sadie, and we set out down our lane, fluffing our feet through the snow. When our lane meets the road, we turn left and walk by the Andersons' farm. Their house is even older than ours — built in 1756 — and I am positive the Andersons share it with at least one ghost. Over the years several people have died in the house, and Mrs. Anderson says that sometimes when she's in the kitchen she can feel another presence in the room, even though no one else is at home. And Sadie will happily go into the Andersons' house, but she refuses to enter their kitchen.

"Let's say hi to Peanut, Sadie," I say.

Peanut is Evvie's horse. She got him on her ninth birthday, which was exactly one year after she turned horse crazy. She stables him at the Andersons'.

Sadie and I wander through the barn. I stop to pat Peanut on his nose. We call hello to the Andersons when we see them sweeping snow off their porch. Then we fluff across their yard and continue down the road.

It is later, after we have turned around and are on our way home, that Santa Claus comes into my head again. Sadie and I are wrapped in this silvery light, the snowflakes whirling around us, no sound but the small howl of the wind. I am looking ahead trying to see our house in the distance, and all of a sudden I can't see anything, anything at all. It is as if Sadie and I are inside a milky bubble. I stop, stand still as a statue, and — for just one teeny moment — I am in a room, a cozy room with a fireplace, a Christmas tree in one corner. And I hear two words in my head. I don't know who says them, but there they are.

Santa Claus.

And then, in another instant, Sadie and I are back in the snow, and I can see the barn and, in the distance, our house, smoke wisping out of the chimney.

"Did you see that?" I ask Sadie. "Did you hear that?" Sadie looks up at me, then down at the snowy road again.

Under all my warm clothes, I shiver.

Two

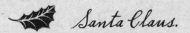 *Santa Claus.*

It is a sign, I think. A sign that I am going to meet the real Santa this year.

I know that Santa comes to our house every Christmas Eve, and I feel I have gone long enough without meeting him. For one thing, I need to talk to him. But also it's actually a little rude — letting him come into our home year after year and leave presents for us, and never thanking him in person. I'm not sure I've ever even written him a thank-you note, although I have thanked him in my heart many, many times.

"Santa," I will say. Or maybe I should address him as Mr. Claus. "Mr. Claus," I will say.

No, too formal. "Santa, it's me, Tess McAlister."

Well, I suppose I don't have to tell him my name. Santa already knows who I am. "Santa, I want to thank you for all the great gifts you have given me."

That's how I think I'll begin. Then I will ask him my questions. And of course I will watch the magic. I have always wondered how, exactly, Santa arrives, and what the magic looks like.

I realize Sadie has stopped walking. She's standing a few feet ahead, staring at me. I have the spooky feeling she knows what I am thinking.

"Sadie, do —" I start to say, but Sadie turns around

then and heads up the lane to our house. So I follow her.

That afternoon I make the mistake of telling Evvie and Maggie about my plan.

Sarah and I have spent two hours making Christmas tree ornaments, two hours talking while we pin and glue and snip and string and paint.

"Why didn't your father come home yesterday?" I ask.

Sarah shrugs. "Something about his blood. They tested it on Thursday and said if it still looked good the next day he could come home for a while. Dr. Evans said he expected it to look good. But when they tested it again it wasn't good after all. So he can't come home yet."

I am about to ask Sarah what she has done with the sign she made when she says, "I folded up his sign and threw it away. I think I'll make him a new one with red and green paper."

"To put up when he comes home for Christmas," I say.

Sarah nods but she doesn't speak, and I see tears in her eyes.

We work quietly. Sarah is painting pieces of macaroni and stringing them onto a length of red yarn. I am making an enormous ornament that I plan to hang near the top of our tree. I am sliding beads and sequins onto hat pins and sticking the pins into a big Styrofoam ball.

I jab a pin into the ball and suddenly say, "Sarah, I have an idea!"

"What?"

"You said your father is on the second floor of the hospital, right?"

"Right."

"And he can see the parking lot from his window, right?"

"Right."

"Then we could visit him sometime. We could stand in the parking lot and sing Christmas songs to him."

Sarah puts down her macaroni chain. "Oh!" she says. "Yes!"

"We could sing 'Rudolph, the Red-Nosed Reindeer' and 'Away in a Manger.'"

"And 'O Little Town of Bethlehem,'" adds Sarah. "That's his favorite."

"We can prepare a whole concert," I say.

"But we might not get to put it on."

"Because he'll probably come home soon."

"But just in case," says Sarah. "We'll plan it just in case."

"We can write up a program that your mother can give your father so he'll know what to expect. Like he's at the theater."

"In case he doesn't come home soon," says Sarah.

"But he probably will."

*   *   *

By four o'clock that afternoon Sarah and I are tired from all of our talking and planning and pinning and gluing and stringing.

"What do you think Evvie and Maggie are doing?" Sarah asks.

"I don't know. They're up in Evvie's room."

"Can we go see?"

On our way up the stairs, I say, "Evvie slept until almost *noon* today."

"Wow," says Sarah.

We stand in the doorway of Evvie's room and see that Maggie is putting curlers in Evvie's hair.

"It takes a long time if you want to do it just right," Maggie is saying importantly. Carefully she combs out a strand of Evvie's hair. Then she takes a brown rubber curler, shaped like an hourglass, from a drawstring bag she has placed on Evvie's dressing table, winds the hair around its skinny middle, folds one half down over the other half, and starts all over again with another strand of hair. Evvie must have ten pounds of curlers bobbling on her head. And Maggie is not done yet.

In the mirror Evvie's eyes shift from herself to Sarah and me. "Hi," she says.

"Hi," we reply.

"What are you two doing?" asks Maggie, looking up from the bag of curlers.

"We were making Christmas ornaments, but we got tired," I tell her.

"Can we watch you?" Sarah asks.

"Sure," says Maggie.

Evvie and Maggie have been extra nice to Sarah lately.

We step into the room, sit on the floor, gape at the girls and the curlers and another bag, which I think might have makeup in it.

"So what's going on?" Maggie asks us.

I glance at Sarah. I know she doesn't want to talk about her father, so I try to think of something interesting to say. And that is when the words that I wish I could take back leave my mouth. "I have decided to meet the real Santa Claus this year."

I see Evvie's eyes meet Maggie's in the mirror. Maggie stifles a laugh. Evvie says, "Really?" And Sarah is staring at me. They are waiting for me to explain.

"Yes. It's really going to happen. I've had a sign."

More stifled giggling from Maggie. But she composes herself. "What kind of sign?" she asks.

I hesitate. I have a feeling that what happened on the walk this morning should be a secret between Sadie and me, that I should not tell anyone about it, not even Sarah.

"Just a sign. But I know what it means."

"And how are you going to see him?" Evvie wants to know. "Stay up until everyone else is asleep, then sneak downstairs and wait?"

Basically, yes. But there is a little more to my plan. I had thought about it until Sarah arrived, and I decided that on Christmas Eve, I will have to be very,

very alert and aware of signs of magic. And I must concentrate on *truly* believing.

All I say, though, is, "Do you think that will work?"

"I guess," answers Sarah. I know that Sarah doesn't believe in Santa any more than Evvie and Maggie do, but she believes in me.

Maggie snorts, but doesn't answer.

Evvie is kinder. "Who knows, Tess?" she replies. "It might work."

I know she thinks I won't be able to stay up; that I'll try and try, then fall asleep and wake up on Christmas morning. Which is what happened when I tried to stay up until midnight on New Year's Eve last year, except that when I woke up it was New Year's Day, of course, not Christmas Day.

But I have my plans, and I have had my sign, and I know I am going to meet Santa Claus.

Three

It is Friday night, nearly a week after my magical sign, when Dad disappears into our attic and returns with a large cardboard carton labeled XMAS LIGHTS. I know what is in there: a big tangled mess of strings and bulbs. The strings with the fat red and green bulbs are for the fir tree in the front yard, and the strings with the tiny gold lights will be for our inside Christmas tree.

Evvie and I are sitting on the floor in the living room cutting strips of red and green construction paper to make into chains for our tree. When I see the XMAS LIGHTS box, I grin. "Look, Evvie. The lights," I say. "Dad, when are we going to get our tree?"

"How about tomorrow?" he replies.

There's a place in Hopewell where the people who live in town buy their trees. But we live far out in the country and we have never bought a tree. We always take our sled and search through the woods behind our house until we find just the right tree, and then we saw it down and pull it home on the sled.

"Can we wait until Sarah gets here," I ask, "so she can come with us?"

"Of course," says Dad.

Mr. Benjamin still has not come home from the hospital. Sarah is going to spend the weekend with us again.

I go back to my chain making. I am so excited that I can't control my hands, and I keep smearing glue all over the strips of paper, causing looks of vague disgust from Evvie. I can't help it. This year I will actually be able to see what Santa thinks of our tree. I want it to be decorated especially beautifully for him.

The next afternoon, Mom and Dad and Evvie and Sarah and I dress in our warmest clothes and set out across our backyard with the sled. Sadie bounds along beside us, leaping through the snow.

"What kind of tree should we look for this year?" asks Dad. "A scrawny, skinny one?"

"No!" Evvie and I cry, and Sarah smiles.

"A little fat one?" asks Mom.

"No, a tall, fat one," I say.

"Not too tall," says Evvie.

"It has to be perfect," I say.

"It should be tall and round and thick, like a tree in a storybook," says Sarah seriously.

We walk deep into the woods.

"How about this one?" asks Dad.

"Not tall enough," I reply.

"There's a big hole in the branches," Sarah points out.

"How about this one?" asks Mom.

"Too thin," says Evvie.

We look and look and look. It takes a long time to find the perfect Christmas tree. Sadie is the one who finally finds it. She sits down in front of a plump fir tree and gives us a doggie grin, her tongue hanging out.

"How about Sadie's tree?" I ask.

"It's tall enough," says Evvie.

"And fat enough," says Mom.

"And just full enough, with no holes," says Dad.

"It's a storybook Christmas tree," says Sarah.

Everyone agrees that it is perfect. So we take turns with the saw until finally the tree rests on its side in the snow.

We lay it on the sled and are about to start home

when Sarah shyly takes Mom's hand and says, "Mrs. McAlister? Look at that tree." She points to a tiny tree, not more than two feet tall. "Could we cut that one down too?"

"To be your Christmas tree?" says Mom. "Don't you think your mother will want to help choose a tree?"

"Oh, yes," replies Sarah. "She will. But I thought she could take this one to Dad. We could even decorate it for him. With little tiny decorations. It's just the right size for his room in the hospital."

"That's a lovely idea, Sarah," says Mom.

So we cut down the tiny tree and add it to the sled. When we finally head back, we are walking in the dusk, snow whirling around us.

"Your dad will probably be home soon," I tell Sarah, "but until then, he can enjoy the little tree."

"I've been thinking," Sarah replies. "Maybe we should start rehearsing our Christmas songs after all, just in case. And we should make the program."

"After we write down the names of the songs we're going to sing, we can decorate the program with pictures of wreaths and holly berries," I say.

Sarah nods.

We walk along in silence. The woods are so quiet that after a while I almost forget where I am. And the next thing I know I am back in that room with the fire and the Christmas tree. Now I see that it is our very own living room. And the tree, the one that is decorated, is the tree we have just found. Exactly the same one.

I shake my head. The vision disappears. It has been another sign, I think. A sign that we have found the perfect Christmas tree, and that when we decorate it, it will make Santa happy. He will whoosh down our chimney, all tired from delivering presents around the world, and there will be a beautiful, glittery, sparkly tree to make him forget, at least for a moment, his aching feet.

I look down and find Sadie trotting along at my

side, looking back up at me. She's wearing that doggie grin again, and for the second time I have the funny feeling that she knows what I've been thinking.

"Christmas Eve, Sadie," I whisper. I'd like to say more, but Sarah is beside me, and anyway Evvie believes it's crazy to talk to animals, and I do not want to do anything to spoil our walk home with our trees.

Four

The days are growing shorter and shorter. In about a week we will have the shortest day of the whole year. It was barely light when Sarah and I got up this morning, and now, in late afternoon, it is already growing dark again.

Mrs. Benjamin has stopped by and picked up Sarah, and Evvie and I are sitting at the table in the kitchen, drinking hot chocolate. I stare out the window, to the back porch and our perfect Christmas tree. When we brought it home yesterday we stood it there in a bucket of water. Now it is waiting to be brought inside and decorated.

I am still gazing out the window when Evvie says to me, "What are you thinking about, Tess? You have the weirdest expression on your face."

What I am thinking right at this very second is that it isn't polite to tell people they look weird, and that Evvie could stand to be a little more tactful. But that sounds rude too, and Santa Claus might be listening. So I say, "I am thinking about Christmas Eve."

"About seeing Santa Claus?" replies Evvie, and I am surprised she remembers.

"Yes," I say cautiously.

"Tess," Evvie begins, and she is using her most annoying big-sister voice. "Tell me . . . how, exactly, do you plan on seeing Santa?"

"I am not just going to see him, I am going to *meet*

him. I'm going to talk with him. I have a whole lot of questions to ask."

"Okay. How do you plan on *meeting* Santa? You can't simply go downstairs and wait for him. Do you know how many kids do that every year? And have you ever heard of one who actually saw Santa?"

I squirm in my seat. I am not squirming because of what Evvie has said. I *know* that when I wait for Santa I will meet him. I am squirming because I do not want to tell Evvie my plan. I think it might jinx the magic.

"Tess?" says Evvie.

"Well . . ."

"I just don't want you to be disappointed on Christmas Day."

I think of something. "Even if I don't see him, it won't mean there isn't a Santa Claus," I say brightly. "It will only mean I didn't see him."

Evvie sighs. She sips elaborately from her mug. "Tess, you really are way too old to believe in Santa

Claus. You know that, don't you? Sarah doesn't believe in him. Just think about this: How could there possibly *be* a Santa? We know where our gifts come from. We buy them for each other. Sarah and Maggie and our other friends drop them off. Nana Florence and Papa Jim mail some."

"But —"

"Even the ones with tags that say they're from Santa," Evvie rushes on, "aren't really from him. They're from Mom and Dad. They just write 'Santa' on the tags for fun. Have we *ever* gotten a present that wasn't actually from Mom or Papa Jim or Sarah or someone?"

I have been waiting for that question. "What about the snow globe?" I ask.

Now it is Evvie's turn to squirm. She twists in her seat. She frowns. I know she knows exactly what I am talking about. It was Christmas morning two years ago. We were opening our presents. And I found one under the tree with a tag that read "For Tess from

Santa. Merry Christmas!" The tag didn't look like any of the tags we had used when we wrapped our presents that year. It was plain white with a small gold star in one corner. The wrapping paper wasn't ours either. But when I opened the box, I turned to Mom and Dad and said, "Thank you, Mom! Thank you, Dad!" anyway.

Mom and Dad looked at each other.

"Isn't this from you?" I asked.

"No," said Mom.

"No," said Dad.

They looked at each other again.

"Evvie?" I said. "Is it from you?"

Evvie shook her head.

"Maybe Nana Florence sent it," I suggested.

But when we called Nana and Papa that night, Nana said the snow globe sounded lovely, but it wasn't from her.

Mom decided Nana Florence must have forgotten she had sent it, but I could tell she didn't believe that.

"It really is from Santa," I announced, wondering just how many of the gifts we receive each year are from Santa — but Mom thinks Dad bought them and Dad thinks Mom bought them, and in all the excitement nobody cares much anyway.

Now Evvie says stubbornly, "The snow globe must have been from *someone*."

"Yeah," I reply. "It was from Santa."

Evvie rolls her eyes. "For heaven's sake." She pauses. "Okay. Tell me this: How does Santa fit enough presents for all the children in the world into one pack and deliver them in a single night? That is not possible."

"Evvie," I begin, "he doesn't need enough presents for *all* the children in the world, only for the ones who celebrate Christmas. And Santa is magic. Anything is possible with magic."

"Santa still has to grant Christmas wishes for absolutely millions of children," Evvie says impatiently. "Besides, what about poor children?"

"What about them?" I ask.

"Why don't they get as many presents as other kids? Santa should be especially nice to them since their parents can't afford to buy toys. He should buy them lots and lots of gifts. But some kids don't get any presents at all. And what about," Evvie rushes on, before I can answer her, "kids like Sarah who wish for things that aren't toys?"

"What do you mean?" I say, even though I know perfectly well what she means.

"I mean that I'm sure Sarah's wish this year is for her father to get better. Do you think Santa can make him well?"

My heart begins to pound. This is exactly why I need to talk to Santa Claus. I consider Evvie's questions. "Well," I say finally, "I think that sometimes, instead of leaving presents, Santa gives the gift of magic to people who need big important things to be done, like finding better houses or getting jobs for the grown-ups. Or making sick people well."

Evvie is giving me a look that I have seen more and

more often on her face since sixth grade began. It is a combination of disgust and disbelief. But she tries to be kind and doesn't say anything. Instead she carries her mug to the sink, rinses it out, and leaves me sitting at the kitchen table.

I look down into my mug and poke at a melted marshmallow. I think about Mr. Benjamin and Santa Claus. I know that Sarah's wish is actually for her father to be able to come home from the hospital in time for Christmas, but I am not sure that Santa can grant wishes *before* Christmas Day. The best I can do is wait until I see Santa on Christmas Eve and ask him please to make Mr. Benjamin well so that he'll be home for Christmas next year.

Five

First thing on Monday morning I open the fifteenth window on my Advent calendar. Under the flap is a picture of one of Santa's elves. My stomach jumps. We are getting closer and closer to Christmas Eve.

I dress in red and green that morning. Green jumper and red blouse with red tights and my saddle shoes.

When Evvie sees me she cries, "Tess, you look like a Christmas elf!"

That is the point.

We hurry to the kitchen.

"Girls," says Mom, "don't take the school bus home this afternoon. I'm going to pick you up. Sarah too. We have to run errands in town."

"My angel wings!" exclaims Evvie.

"Yes, we'll go to the sewing store," says Mom.

Every year the kids at our church put on a Christmas pageant, the Nativity. Every year I love watching it, and every year Evvie loves being in it. I have never been in it. I do not like being stared at. But Evvie has been in it year after year. She has played a sheep and a cow and a shepherd and a goat and another sheep. This year, though, she is going to be the angel Gabriel. And Maggie is going to be Mary. For the last three weeks, whenever Evvie and Maggie have not been curling their hair or whispering about Dan Soderberg, who is the cutest boy in their class, they have been rehearsing their roles in the pageant. Since they don't have to say any lines, Evvie has been practicing waving her arms and looking angelic, and Maggie has been practicing holding a baby and looking holy.

Evvie wants her Gabriel costume to be perfect. And we have to make a new one, because last year's angel, Carl Hatley, was two years older and eight inches taller than Evvie. His costume will never fit her. Evvie wants gossamer wings and a gold halo and, if possible, to look as though she is standing in a cloud.

"We'd better go to the hobby shop too," Evvie says. "We need gold wire and sparkles."

"Do you need to do any Christmas shopping, Tess?" Mom asks.

"A little," I reply. I am making most of my presents in school. That is what we do all December in art class. I am making candy dishes for Mom and Nana Florence, and pencil cups for Dad and Papa Jim, and a headband for Evvie.

But I still need presents for Sarah and Sadie. And

something for Santa. I have decided that since I am going to meet Santa, it would be nice to give him a gift — something better than the cookies and hot chocolate I always leave for him. Probably everybody leaves him cookies and hot chocolate. There is Santa flying around the world dropping off wonderful gifts, and what does he get in return but plates of cookies and gallons of hot chocolate. I bet he can't stand cookies and hot chocolate by now. I want to give him something else.

"Mom, can Sarah and I shop by ourselves while you and Evvie get the things for her costume?"

"Certainly," replies Mom.

"Goody." I love going into town at Christmastime. Everything is lit with tiny gold lights. The lampposts are wound with green garlands and red ribbons. And the store windows . . . I could look in them forever. They'll be full of stars and wreaths and angels and Santas and reindeer and elves and snowmen and tinsel and bows. The window of the toy shop is my favorite. Mr. Vinsel fills it with moving toys — an electric train, a twirling ballerina doll, marionettes that somehow dance all by themselves, a Santa who waves his hands, a little black dog that jumps up and down. Plus, Mr. Vinsel plays Christmas music, so you can look and look and look in the window while you listen to "Hark! The Herald Angels Sing" and "It Came upon a Midnight Clear" and "Jingle Bells."

In town that afternoon Sarah and I wave good-bye to Mom and Evvie. Then we walk down the street, pausing to gaze into every window.

I have four dollars and eighty-one cents in my change purse, which I think will be enough for three presents. "I need to buy a present for Sadie and one for you," I tell Sarah. (I do not mention the present for Santa.) "You can come with me to the pet store, but not to Jensen's, okay?"

Sarah grins. "Okay. While you go to Jensen's, I'll go to the Fir Tree. No spying! We'll meet at Mr. Vinsel's window later."

"Perfect," I say.

At Noah's Ark, Sarah helps me choose a bag of dog cookies for Sadie. Then she goes to the Fir Tree, and I scuff along the snowy sidewalk to Jensen's. When I step inside, I stamp my feet on the mat, then head straight for the dollhouse furniture. I have decided to get a Christmas tree for Sarah's dollhouse. I know she has wanted one for a long time. I choose one with tiny decorations and lights on it. I am about to carry it to the counter when I see something that I know will be the perfect gift for Santa.

It's a snow globe. But inside the globe, in all the whirling snow, is a springtime scene — a garden in bloom. It's a funny scene for a snow globe, but I think Santa will like it. For one thing, he probably never gets to see spring flowers up at the North Pole. Also, the snow globe will be my way of telling him that I know about the other snow globe, the one he left for me two years ago. The one that was a clue that Santa is real.

When I have paid for the snow globe and the Christmas tree, I have only fourteen cents left — one dime and four pennies. But I don't care. My Christmas shopping is finished, and I know I have gotten just the right gifts. Well, I know Sarah's and Santa's gifts are right. But I am not certain about the cookies I have chosen for Sadie. It is so hard to know what to buy for a dog.

That night I carry a roll of wrapping paper and a spool of red ribbon to my room, close the door, and wrap all my Christmas gifts. I love Christmas secrets, even the ones that aren't magic. When the gifts are wrapped, I line them up on my bed and stare at them.

"This is the beginning," I whisper. It is the beginning of absolutely the most Christmasy time of all December. And this year it is when I begin to hurtle toward Christmas Eve and Santa and the magic.

On Tuesday Sarah rides the bus home with me after school, and we plan the carol program for her father.

On Wednesday night Dad brings our perfect Christmas tree inside, and he and Mom and Evvie and I decorate it. We unpack our decorations from their old boxes and admire the new decorations I made with Sarah, and we drink hot chocolate and sing "O Christmas Tree." I get to put the star on top of the tree, and Evvie gets to plug in the lights. When she does, Dad turns off all the lamps in the living room and we look at our tree, shining in the dark. It is the tree from my Christmas visions.

On Thursday Sarah comes home with me again, and she and Evvie and Mom and I bake batches and batches of Christmas cookies — gingerbread men and bells and stars and reindeer and Santas. Our kitchen is warm, and our house smells of spices. We put the cookies into tins, one for the Andersons, one for Evvie's teacher, one for my teacher, one for Sarah and her mother, one for us, and one for Sarah's father.

On Friday when Sarah rides the bus home with me,

she is carrying her suitcase. She will be with us until Sunday. She doesn't say much. There are only six days left until Christmas. The tiny tree has been set up in Mr. Benjamin's hospital room, and we will put the program on for him the next day. Mom has said she will drive us to the hospital.

When Sarah and Evvie and I step off the bus that afternoon, Mom is waiting for us with Sadie, who is wearing a giant red bow around her neck. Evvie and I laugh when we see her, but Sarah bursts into tears.

"Come on, honey," says Mom, and she takes Sarah's suitcase from her, then holds her hand while we walk to the house.

Evvie and I do everything we can think of to cheer up Sarah. Finally Evvie invites Maggie over, and they put on their costumes and give us a secret performance of their roles in the pageant.

"Ooh, your wings look *real*!" Sarah exclaims when she sees the Gabriel costume.

"And you look so . . . so mothery," I tell Maggie.

"Do I look holy?" she asks.

"Oh, yes," Sarah and I assure her.

By Saturday Sarah seems more cheerful.

"Are you ready for our program?" she asks me.

"All ready," I reply.

"Could I be part of it?" asks Evvie, and I feel bad that we didn't think to ask her to join us.

Sarah and I look at each other. "You could be our backup singer," Sarah says.

"Okay," replies Evvie.

When we arrive at the hospital, Mom parks the car, then runs inside with the program for Mr. Benjamin. "I'll call down to you in a few minutes, girls," she says.

Sarah and Evvie and I climb out of the car and look at the hospital.

"Do you know which window is your dad's?" Evvie asks Sarah.

"Yup." She points it out. "Okay, now we have to get ready. Evvie, you stand behind Tess and me. I'm going to announce each song before we sing it. That way, you'll know what's coming up, okay?"

"Okay," says Evvie. She'll do anything Sarah says.

We are gazing at the window Sarah has pointed out, blowing on our hands, when suddenly the window opens and I can see Sarah's father in it. He's wearing a bathrobe, and even from our distance, even standing down here in the parking lot, I can see that his face is gaunt, almost like a skeleton's, and that his hands are shaking.

"Dad! Hi, Dad!" cries Sarah, and it is as if a light has been turned on somewhere and is shining only on Sarah's face.

"Hi, Mr. Benjamin," Evvie and I say. "Merry Christmas!"

Mr. Benjamin gives us a wave. "Hi, girls," he says. "Merry Christmas." He speaks so softly that it's hard to hear him. But then he holds up the program, and I see the grin on his face.

Sarah looks at Evvie and me. "Hit it," she exclaims. And we begin the show with "Away in a Manger."

Mr. Benjamin's smile grows bigger. By the time we have sung the last verse of "O Little Town of Bethlehem," which is the end of our show, Mr. Benjamin is holding a handkerchief to his eyes, but he is still smiling. "That," he says, "was the most wonderful Christmas present I could imagine. Thank you."

Later, when Mom is driving Sarah and Evvie and me home, the countryside flying by outside the windows of the car, I turn to look at Sarah. I see a small smile on her lips, and I know she is thinking of her father and our Christmas show.

Six

❦ *The days after Saturday* are slow but delicious, like chocolate melting on my tongue. Our mailman arrives with packages wrapped in brown paper and tied with string. DO NOT OPEN UNTIL CHRISTMAS! is written on them. One from Nana Florence and Papa Jim in Winter Park, Florida; one from Aunt Adele and Uncle Paul in Louisville, Kentucky; one from Dad's cousins in Fort Smith, Arkansas. A small box arrives that says OPEN RIGHT NOW! That is the fruitcake Aunt Martha makes every year. It weighs a ton. I am the only person in our family who likes it.

On Monday night, which is the night before our last day of school, Evvie and I are putting the finishing touches on Christmas cards for our classmates when we hear sweet clear voices singing "Angels We Have Heard on High." I am so startled, and so certain of the magic I will soon see, that at first I think angels really are outside our house, that if Evvie and I run to the windows, we will see angels adrift in the clouds and snow in the inky sky, singing ancient words. But then, "Christmas carolers!" cries Evvie.

Where have they come from? We live so far out in the country. Evvie is right, though. She flings open our front door, and we find nine people gathered outside, bundled into their warmest clothes, their breath frosty, and their voices raised as they sing another carol. They are from our church, I realize, and when they finish singing, Mom invites them inside for hot chocolate and our homemade cookies.

Tuesday is the last day of school before vacation. My classmates and I do not get much work done. Miss Sullivan is patient with us. She reads a Christmas story called *The Tailor of Gloucester*, reads it to us from behind her desk, which is piled with the tins of cookies and small wrapped packages we have brought her. Then we hand around the cards and things we have been making for each other.

At the end of the day I call good-bye to Sarah. Mr. Benjamin's doctor has decided that Sarah's father is to be allowed home until December 26th, and Sarah is trembling with excitement as she waits for her bus.

"Good-bye, good-bye! Merry Christmas!" Sarah calls back.

Later Evvie and I jump off the school bus. As we run along our lane, Sadie comes flying through the snow to greet us, as if she knows it is a special day.

The three of us burst through our front door and into the house, which smells of gingerbread and feels like secrets.

I awaken the next morning with butterflies dancing in my stomach and lie in the gray glow of another snowy morning. Tonight the magic will be revealed to me. I wonder how it will begin, what the first sign will be.

And I wonder this all day, which makes the twenty-fourth of December seem even longer than usual. But that's okay because this is one of the last chances for looking at the wrapped gifts under the tree, for waiting for friends to drop by for a Christmas visit, for dreaming of the magic.

Late in the afternoon, as darkness is falling, I notice that the snow has stopped. The sky has cleared and the stars are out.

"Time to get ready for church, Tess," calls Mom, and I run to my room to change into a dress. Evvie is already in her room. She is putting on the clothes she will wear under her angel costume, and assembling her wings and things in two brown paper bags.

Quietly I close the door to my room. Then I turn off the light, stand at my window, and look outside into the dusk. I am standing there, my eyes fixed on the sky above the Andersons' barn, when I feel something — a shift in the atmosphere, barely noticeable. But I draw in my breath, and the air around me seems to crinkle and the stars to shine brighter. I get the same shivery feeling I have when the lights dim at the movie theater. Something is happening.

"Tess?" Dad calls.

"Coming!" I call back.

I wriggle into the black velvet dress that Nana Florence made for me, pull on white tights and red shoes, and run downstairs.

Mom and Dad and Evvie and I pile into the car, and Dad drives us through the countryside and into town.

We sing "Winter Wonderland" and I try to recite "The Night Before Christmas," but I get stuck at the part about the luster of midday and the objects below.

By the time we are parking behind the church, Evvie's teeth are chattering, and she says she's not cold, she's nervous.

"But Evvie," I say, "you are the most realistic angel I have ever seen. Your halo really looks like it's floating over your head. And everyone will be able to imagine that you're standing in a cloud."

"Thank you," says Evvie. *Chatter, chatter, chatter.* She is always nervous just before the pageant begins.

Inside, the church is warm and smells of evergreens. The Advent candles flicker and glow. Everyone is dressed up, and the little children are going to real church instead of Sunday school, so they are hushed and excited, standing in the pews until their parents tell them to sit down.

"I'll see you later," whispers Evvie as she rushes off with her costume.

Mom and Dad and I walk along the stone floor of the church, down the aisle, and find seats in the fourth row of pews. I look at the place where our minister usually stands and talks. The pulpit is gone, and the front of the church is so dark that I can't even read the words about Our Savior that I know are written there. I am peaceful, then excited as that shivery feeling comes over me again.

In the balcony behind us the organ starts to play. I hear the first notes of "Silent Night." Everyone quiets down, even the smallest children, and when the music stops, a soft light is shone on the front of the church. Suddenly in all that quiet we hear a great clatter from behind the closed door near where the pulpit should be. Then we hear, "Oof." A moment later the door is flung open and through it walk Maggie in her Mary costume, Walter Shaw in his Joseph costume, and a bumbling donkey, played by two kids in one costume. They are having a lot of trouble moving together all bent over inside the fake gray fur, and they trip going through the door. They trip again as they stumble along behind Maggie, so that she bumps into Walter, and for just a second the holy look leaves her face and is replaced by a crabby look. I glance at Dad sitting next to me and see that he is trying not to laugh.

After that, though, Maggie's holy look returns, and the narrator, Lydia Bloom, begins to read the passages from the Bible that tell the story of the first Christmas. Everything goes smoothly as the innkeeper shows Mary and Joseph and their donkey to the stable. The light dims then, and when it is turned up again, Mary and Joseph and the stable animals have been replaced by shepherds and their sheep.

This is when Evvie will appear. I know she wishes she could make her entrance by flying over the heads of the shepherds, but that is not possible. She must content herself with standing quietly in the darkness apart from the shepherds, then having a light suddenly illuminate her, catching the sparkles on her wings and making her glow like the Advent candles. It is a startling appearance if you didn't know it was going to happen, and I think it is almost as good as flying down from the ceiling.

The rest of the pageant goes fine except for the fight that breaks out between two of the shepherds, and except for the fact that the Jesus doll looks like a girl.

When the pageant is over, the organ starts to play again and we sing three carols, including "O Holy Night," which is Dad's favorite. Then we walk slowly out of the church, greeting people as we go. We wait for Evvie by the stone steps and soon here she comes, running to us, wearing her regular clothes, but with the halo still bobbing on her head because she can't bear to take it off yet.

"You were wonderful," we tell Evvie, and she grins.

Then Mom says, "Who's ready for dinner?"

"We are!" cry Evvie and I, and we drive through the dark streets of Hopewell to the Coach Room, where we meet Uncle Rick and Aunt Merlena and our cousins Carolyn and Peter. They live not far away, in Falls Village, and every year we have Christmas Eve dinner together in the Coach Room.

"We're eating in town!" crows Evvie, halo jiggling.

"Mom, can we have Coke?" I ask.

"If you promise it won't keep you awake tonight."

"No, no, it won't," I say, hoping it will, and deciding to order a large one.

Dad parks the car in Palmer Square, and soon we are hurrying into the restaurant, greeting our cousins.

"Merry Christmas!" everyone calls.

"I'm going to have french fries!" says Evvie, which is an eating-in-town treat.

"I'm going to have a cheeseburger," I say.

"No clam chowder?" asks Dad.

Evvie and Carolyn and Peter and I hold our noses

and shake our heads, which reminds Evvie to remove her halo.

Later, when our town dinner is over and we are all full and happy, but too excited to be sleepy, we say good-bye to our cousins and wish them merry Christmas again, and soon Mom and Dad and Evvie and I are driving home.

We know just what to do when we get there. Evvie and I run to our rooms and change into our night-gowns while Dad makes a firc in the fireplace, and Mom turns on the tree lights and finds our old copy of "The Night Before Christmas." The four of us sit in front of the fire, Sadie dozing with her head in my lap. We take turns reading the story of Santa's visit, and then we hang our stockings.

"Cookies for Santa?" says Mom then, and Evvie rolls her eyes, but I fix a plate for him, thinking instead of the present I have bought, the one I can give him myself later tonight.

At last Evvie and I climb the stairs to our rooms, leaving Sadie asleep before the fire. I slip under my covers and lie in bed. I have pulled the window shade up so I can see outside. The moon is full, the stars are still shining, and I think I hear a low hum. It is all around me. My heart pounds as the magic unfolds.

In two and a half hours I will meet Santa Claus.

Seven

I know I will not have any trouble staying awake until midnight. Large Coke or no large Coke, I will not fall asleep tonight before I meet Santa. The magic is building all around me, building toward midnight. The hum is growing louder, and sounds seem to be sharpened and softened at the same time. I hear chirps and clucks and wings fluttering. I can even hear the horses stomping their feet in the Andersons' barn. But I hear all these things in a muted way that makes me think the world is wrapped in gauze. Outside my window I see millions and millions of pinprick stars, and birds roosting on every branch of every tree. I have never felt the magic so strongly before, and I do not want to miss a moment of it.

I lie on my bed again, rest my hands under my head, and feel my flannel nightgown against my legs. I listen to the sounds from downstairs. I am pretty sure I know what Mom and Dad are doing. Now that Evvie and I are in bed, they are putting the presents under the tree — all those presents that have been arriving in the mail, and others our parents have bought and hidden in the house. I know where their hiding place is. Evvie discovered it three years ago. It's very clever — a box way back in a corner of our attic. The box is huge. It's a cardboard wardrobe, and it's labeled WINTER COATS, which sounds pretty boring. I think it actually does hold our winter coats in the summer, but it's empty in the winter — except when Mom and

Dad hide things in it that they don't want Evvie and me to see.

Sure enough, just after the clock in the living room chimes once for ten-thirty, I hear footsteps climbing upstairs, walking along the hallway, then, after the door to the attic opens, climbing another flight. A few minutes later, the footsteps return to the living room, then make a second trip to the attic. I picture Dad with his arms piled with wrapped gifts. Some of those gifts bear tags that read "To Evvie from Mom" or "For Tess from Mom and Dad," but other tags, I am quite sure, say "For Tess from Santa Claus" or "To Evvie from Santa" — in Mom's handwriting.

I slip out of bed and tiptoe across the chilly room to the door, where I put my ear to the crack and listen. I can hear Christmas carols on the radio. I imagine Mom and Dad taking a break, sitting in front of the fire, maybe sipping tea. Soon, I know, they will fill the stockings. Later, Santa will add a few things of his own to the stockings, of course. And I suppose he will add a present or two to the pile under the tree, although in the excitement tomorrow, Mom and Dad and Evvie probably won't realize that they actually are from Santa.

But I will know.

I dash across my room again, my feet beginning to feel like ice cubes. For the next half hour I simply lie in bed and listen, or sit up and look out the window. It seems to me that each time I gaze across the snow to the Andersons' barn, the sky above it is a bit brighter.

I'm kneeling on my bed looking out the window again, when our house grows quieter. Mom and Dad have turned off the radio. There are no more sounds coming from the living room. But suddenly there are footsteps in the hallway.

In a flash I scurry under the covers, turn onto my stomach, face the wall, close my eyes, and breathe deeply. When the door to my room opens, I am as still as the moon. Light from the hallway falls across my face as someone peeps in at me, then closes the door quietly. I do not move again until I am certain Mom and Dad are in bed and sound asleep.

The clock chimes eleven-thirty.

I throw the covers back and kneel once more at the window. I open it slightly, even though the air is absolutely freezing. I tiptoe to my closet, put on my bathrobe, then return to the window. The most powerful magic is almost here, and now I must pay close attention to everything.

I breathe in the winter air, breathe in deeply, then let my breath out in cloudy puffs. The air is crisp; it is clean and sharp. I let my eyes travel across the snow, across the road, and again to the sky above the Andersons' barn. And my eyes light on an enormous star. I have never seen it before. It is rising and rising, and as I watch, it finally settles so that it appears to hover just a few feet above the barn, making the barn seem to glow as if it were lit from inside instead of outside.

I turn back to my room and hear the hum, louder now, then face the window again. In the distance I hear bells. Sleigh bells, I think, and then I realize I hear church bells too, chiming out carols and hymns and ancient tunes. The birds begin to leave the trees, and a dove flies by my window, a white dove from a fairy tale or a picture book. It moves lazily, turning to look at me for a moment, then continues its slow flight — around our house twice, then gently, as if it's floating, across our yard, and across the road to the barn, where it perches on the roof.

Ting, ting, ting, ring the sleigh bells.

Gloria in excelsis Deo, chime the church bells.

Go tell it on the mountain. A voice whispers this near my ear, and I jump, startled. I turn around, but no one is in my room. The hum is fading, though, I notice, and in its place, all around me, just in the air, are little murmurings and mutterings and snippets of songs.

Love came down at Christmas . . .

The boar's head, as I understand, is the rarest dish in all this land . . .

Wassail, wassail, all over the town! . . .

In the bleak midwinter, long ago . . .

Peace on the earth, good will to men . . .

I take one last look outside — at the brilliant star; at the glowing barn; at the sky, which is now filled with birds; at our yard, in which I see chipmunks and squirrels chattering away, a family of pheasants hurrying along, and four deer (the regular kind, not reindeer) who look as though they are holding a conversation.

I close the window, shutting out the icy air, but after I do, I can still hear the bells and the songs and the voices on the wind. I turn and start to slide off of my bed, but leap backward when I see Sadie sitting by my desk, her head cocked to the side. How did she get into my room? The door is open, but I know Mom and Dad closed it before they went to bed.

"Sadie?" I say, and she cocks her head to the other side. "Sadie, how did you open the door?" She pulls her lips back in a doggie grin, stands up, and shakes herself.

Moving slowly and carefully, I open the top drawer of my desk and take out the snow globe I bought for Santa. I have decided not to wrap it. I want to show it to Santa and explain why I chose it for him. I have arranged it in a box, though, a box lined with tissue paper, so the globe won't break as Santa goes flying around the world.

Then I take one last look out the window, just long enough to see that hundreds of birds — doves and sparrows and cardinals and chickadees and others I can't identify — have arranged themselves in rows on the barn roof, covering it like feathered shingles. Their loud chatter sounds almost like words, but I can't understand what they're saying.

"Come on, Sadie," I whisper. "Let's go downstairs and wait for Santa. We have to be very quiet, though, okay?"

I step silently into the hallway, pause, and listen. Evvie's door is closed. So is the door to Mom and Dad's room. I reach down and rest my hand on Sadie's warm head, and we tiptoe along the hallway, then step cautiously down the stairs. The living room is as I had expected it would be. The fire in the hearth is only glowing embers now. Above it hang our stockings, already stuffed by Mom and Dad. And under the tree is a pile of presents. I reach down, read a few of the tags. "For Tess from Sarah." "To Evvie, love Aunt Adele and Uncle Paul." And sure enough, "Merry Christmas to Tess from Santa" in what I am certain is Mom's handwriting.

I peek through the window and look out at the yard. The animals I saw there earlier are now moving toward the barn, joined by others. The star shines as brightly as ever, and the ringing and chiming and songs and words are everywhere. Indoors, outdoors, in my head. I hear one particularly loud voice:

And this shall be the sign:
The heavenly Babe you there shall find
To human view displayed,
All meanly wrapped in swathing bands,
And in a manger laid.

I look at Sadie, who is looking back at me with contented squinty eyes. "What? Tell me what is going to happen," I say. "You know, don't you?"

Sadie flops down onto her haunches, her tongue hanging out. I flop down into an armchair. It is near the Christmas tree, and it faces the fireplace. The box with the snow globe rests in my lap. I look at the clock on the mantel. Ten minutes until midnight.

I settle back and wait.

Eight

The hands on the clock move closer to midnight. As they do, the room seems to grow noisier and noisier. I must be the only human in our house who can hear the din, though. The murmurings and mutterings have become loud voices, the songs now offered up by entire choirs. In all the noise, though, I feel only peace.

I gaze into the fireplace. I am staring at the red and

orange embers when a gust of wind comes whooshing down the chimney, roaring and whistling and bringing with it dry leaves and a swirl of snow.

Eleven fifty-nine.

With a loud pop and a shower of sparks, the fire springs to life again. Soon it is crackling away, as big a blaze as when we hung our stockings hours earlier.

I grip the arms of the chair. For the first time I feel just the teensiest bit afraid, afraid of what, exactly, I will see tonight. I do not think that on the dot of midnight Santa will slide down the chimney — that will happen later. But something is about to happen, and I don't know what. I look outside at the star, at the birds on the roof of the barn, at the animals streaming toward the barn. I listen to the music, the songs, the bells. A voice, loud but clear and pure, sings over and over again, "What happiness befalls me, what happiness befalls me."

And the clock chimes twelve.

It is midnight on Christmas Eve.

I glance at Sadie, then gasp and sit up straight as a wavery form appears above the hearth. The form shimmers and begins to take shape. I see wings, a gown, a head, and above the head, what must be a halo, although it looks absolutely nothing like the halo Evvie fashioned for her pageant costume.

There is an angel in our living room.

But only for a moment.

Just as I let out a small cry, the angel fades away. I am on my feet now, breathing hard.

Sadie is on her feet too. She stands beside me, looks up at me with her gentle eyes, and says, "Don't be afraid, Tess."

I can't answer. Sadie has spoken to me, and I am speechless.

And then . . . and then I remember old stories, things I have read in books, something about the animals being able to talk on Christmas Eve. Why has this never occurred to me? That in this time of wonder and magic, Sadie would be able to speak, that I could talk to her and she could answer me, just as I've wished for so long.

"Sadie?" I whisper, sinking back into the chair. I no longer feel afraid.

Sadie jumps into my lap and looks into my eyes, her snout inches from my face. "It's Christmas magic," she replies, and her voice is smooth and low, not quite a growl, not quite human.

I can't think what to say next. I have been waiting three years to be able to talk with Sadie. I've told her secrets, told her my scary dreams in the middle of the night, complained to her about school problems when I walked with her down our lane. Now here she is sitting in my lap, telling me about Christmas magic. And I say to her, "Sadie, you can talk! Are we feeding you the right kind of food?"

Sadie laughs. "The right kind of food? I suppose it's all right. As dog food goes."

I laugh too. "I can't — I never — I was thinking so much about Santa — I mean, I didn't think about any other Christmas magic. I just thought I'd see Santa Claus come down the chimney tonight. I never dreamed anything else would happen. . . . How long will you be able to talk?"

"For a while," says Sadie.

"Can you talk every Christmas Eve?"

Sadie nods her head.

"Why haven't I ever heard you?"

"Because you weren't ready to hear me. You are a believer, Tess, but this year you let yourself receive the magic. It's inside you now."

I nod. I don't so much understand this as *feel* it.

"Sadie . . ." I pause, thinking of all I want to ask her. "Sadie, where did you come from? How did you get into that ditch when you were a puppy?"

"I was born in the woods," she replies. "The woods you go to when you look for your Christmas trees. My mother had two pups — my sister and me. She left us one day and was hit by a car, I think. Someone found my sister just before you found me."

"Did your mother give you another name?" I ask. "Maybe Sadie isn't your proper name."

"Sadie is a fine name," she says, "but my mother named me River. Dog mothers name their puppies for things that are important to them. You can call me Sadie, though."

I scratch her ears and tell her solemnly, "You are one of my best friends, you know."

"Thank you. I do know that," says Sadie, and she presses her paw into my hand.

"Oh!" I exclaim. "You mean . . . you can understand me even when you can't answer?"

"Yes."

"Do you understand everything we say to you all year long?"

"Yes."

"So I can talk to you anytime, and you'll understand me?"

"Yes," answers Sadie. She shifts position in my lap, but her eyes hold mine steadily.

Something wonderful occurs to me. "Do you get to see the Christmas magic every year?" Sadie nods her head. "Do all animals see it?" I ask. She nods again. "And can they talk every year?"

"Yes. But most humans can't hear them."

"Do you see the angel?" I go on. "And hear the bells and the singing —"

"Yes. It's all part of the Christmas magic," Sadie tells me patiently. "Think about what happened on the first Christmas, the Christmas in the stable. And think about what has happened on Christmases since then. Everything comes together each year: past and present, ancient and new."

"The magic," I say, trying to understand. "What happened on the first Christmas — was that magic?"

Sadie looks thoughtful. "No," she says slowly, "not magic. A miracle, I suppose. But it's magic now that keeps —" Sadie stops speaking suddenly, straightens, and cocks her head to the right.

"What is it?" I ask, my heart quickening.

"Shh," says Sadie softly. Then, "Listen. Do you hear it, Tess?"

I realize that over all the other sounds, I now hear a sharp jingling of bells, which drowns out the other bells and the voices and music and songs.

"The sleigh bells?" I ask.

"Yes!" cries Sadie, jumping off of my lap. She runs to our front door. "Tess, hurry! Get ready. Santa Claus is about to arrive."

Nine

I look at Sadie in amazement. "How do you know?" I ask.

"I see him every year," she answers. "The sleigh bells are his signal. Now hurry, Tess!"

"But what am I supposed to do?"

"Put on your coat and boots. And unlock the front door."

"Do I have time?"

"Yes. Just hurry!"

I grab my coat out of the hall closet and pull on Evvie's boots, which are the first pair I can find. Then, with trembling hands, I turn the lock on the door.

When I open the door Sadie dashes ahead of me, out into the yard. I close the door quietly behind us, then hurry after her. She is standing in the middle of the yard, face turned upward, and I lift my face as well.

I see the clear deep sky, the pinpoints of starlight. I think I see the wisp of angel wings too, and I hear nothing but sleigh bells, so loud now that I put my hands over my ears.

"There!" cries Sadie, pointing upward with one paw.

And in a whirl of sparkles and mist, a magnificent sleigh — gold and red, all graceful curves and curlicues, and shining like the stars — appears in the sky just over the roof of our house. It is pulled by a team of reindeer, and as I watch, it makes a smooth landing next to our chimney.

It's just like in books, I think. Just exactly like in "The Night Before Christmas," and I realize then that of course other people have seen the magic over the years. Maybe Mr. Clement C. Moore himself even saw the magic, and that is how he wrote about it so well.

I nudge Sadie. "Did —"

Sadie hushes me. "Keep watching," she says.

I turn back to the roof. The reindeer are standing patiently now. They are a team of eight — two and two and two and two. And they pause nobly, their fine antlers glistening with snow. They paw at the roof, their harness bells jingling, but not as loudly now that they are standing still.

I stand on tiptoe and try to get a better look at the sleigh. The inside is crimson-colored velvet, and stuffed into the back is a pack so enormous that it's spilling over the sides of the sleigh. I wish I could see inside the pack, but it's tied together tightly at the top with a crimson cord. Santa's reins are silver, and so are the sleigh bells.

And Santa is . . . It's funny, but I can't decide what size he is. He looks like a giant and an elf all at once. He's round, of course, with a white beard, and the suit is pretty much what I expected — red with white trim and gold buttons and a wide black belt. His mittens are green, though, and I wonder if he has many suits, if he has a whole wardrobe of suits, each one a little different from the others.

As I watch, Santa drops the reins with a jingle, stands, and climbs out of the sleigh. Then he turns and reaches for the pack. It looks as though it should weigh a ton, but Santa lifts it out as lightly as if it were empty. Then he throws it over his back and steps toward our chimney.

I feel Sadie's cold nose on my bare hand then, and I look down at her.

"Come on, Tess," she whispers. "Back inside now. You don't want to miss the best part."

Sadie is already trotting toward the front door, and after one more glance at the spectacle on our roof — this spectacle that apparently only Sadie and I can see and hear — I hurry after her.

I follow Sadie into our living room, where she positions herself behind the armchair I was sitting in. From there we have a good view of the fireplace, but we won't be seen.

We direct our attention to the hearth. I have just realized that the fire is still blazing away, and I draw in my breath, ready to exclaim something to Sadie, when she places one furry paw on my arm, cautioning me to be quiet.

My eyes are fixed on the fire. I can't look away from it. I am sure that Santa is going to slide down our chimney and land in the flames, and so my breath comes in small gasps and I grip Sadie's paw tightly.

And then I feel another gust of wind. It seems to come from outside, from above me, from all around. It brings a shower of Santa's sparkling mist down the chimney, and suddenly, I don't know quite how, there is Santa in our living room. The fire blazes behind him, and he stands unharmed — not burned or singed — on our hearth. In fact, he looks a bit chilly. He's rubbing his mittened hands together, and there's a dusting of snow on his shoulders and hat.

Santa Claus glances around our living room, and I have just realized that he is not holding his pack, when down the chimney it comes all by itself, and lands — also unharmed — at Santa's feet.

"Ah, very good," says Santa softly, and loosens the crimson cord. He rummages around in the pack, pulling out small items. He looks at each one intently, and then either puts it back or sets it at his feet. Presently, he stoops to examine the items he has chosen. I see a game of jacks, a puzzle, a tiny kaleidoscope, an even tinier book. Santa drops one into each of our stockings.

Then he turns to the pack again and begins to remove larger presents from it. These are wrapped and bear tags. I realize that no matter how many things Santa takes out of the pack, it seems to remain as full as ever.

"Hmm, Evvie," Santa mutters, placing a gift under our tree. "Growing up . . . Paints should be all right . . . Monopoly for Tess . . ."

Now that I can see Santa up close, I decide that he is neither a giant nor an elf. Here in our living room he looks neither particularly tall nor particularly short. What I can't decide now is how old he is. He has that long white beard and some wrinkles too, but somehow he doesn't look elderly. Papa Jim looks older than Santa. Santa is spry and moves quickly as he stoops and rummages and darts between the pack and the tree.

After Santa has carefully placed two gifts among those already under our tree, and written something on their tags, he returns the other presents to the pack and draws the cord tight. Then he looks around our living room again. This time he sees the plate of cookies and the mug of hot chocolate (which must be cold by now) that I left for him on a table near the fireplace. He politely takes a sip from the mug, pats a few drops of hot chocolate from his mustache, then eats a cookie shaped like a snowman.

"Tasty," he murmurs. "Very tasty indeed. And a beautifully decorated tree," he adds. "Quite lovely."

Then, just like in Mr. Moore's story, Santa stands by the fireplace and lays his finger beside his nose.

Is he leaving? Is he leaving already?

Santa is about to nod his head when Sadie pushes me from behind the armchair. Still wearing Evvie's boots and my coat, I stumble out into the room.

Santa turns and sees me.

"Aha," he says. "Christmas magic."

Ten

For a moment I can do nothing but stare at Santa. I can't decide what to say to him, and I'm not even sure how I should feel. I'm excited, of course, but is it all right to have spied on Santa? Will he mind? I can't imagine Santa getting angry, but you never know.

"Excuse me, Mr. Claus, sir," I begin, and then I am

aware of Sadie stepping out from behind the arm-chair. She stands next to me, leaning against my leg.

"There you are, Sadie," says Santa. "Merry Christmas."

"Merry Christmas," replies Sadie, her mouth widening into her grin. She leaves my side and crosses the floor to Santa Claus, sits before him, and raises her paw. Santa takes it between his hands.

"So," says Santa, "another year."

Sadie nods. "Another year. And here is Tess."

"Did you have to help her much?"

"Not at all. She let the magic in all by herself. It was especially important to her this year."

Santa regards me seriously.

I find my voice. "Santa, did you know I would see you this year?"

"I believed you would see me sometime soon."

"I've been waiting all my life to meet you," I say. "And to see the Christmas magic."

"Finding the magic is a wonderful thing, Tess."

"Once someone has found the magic, does she always have it?" I ask.

"Not always. But usually."

I think of what I must talk to Santa about, but then I remember the important thing I want to do, and I say, "Santa, I have something for you." I retrieve the box containing the snow globe from the table next to the armchair. I don't remember setting it there, but I must have done so when the angel appeared and I leapt to my feet. "You've given me so many things," I tell Santa, "but I've never given you anything. Except cookies and cold hot chocolate, which you must get tons of. So this year I want to give you a present." I hand the box to him. "Merry Christmas," I say.

"Why, thank you," replies Santa, and he's looking at me with eyes that are both twinkling and serious. He removes the lid from the box, pulls aside the tissue paper, and lifts out the snow globe, holding it in his hand for a moment. Slowly he turns the globe upside down, then right side up, and watches the snow fall on the tiny garden of daffodils and hyacinths.

"It's so you can see spring flowers, even at the North Pole," I tell him.

Santa smiles at me. "This is a very thoughtful gift, Tess."

"You can leave it in the box, so it won't get broken while you're flying around," I point out.

"I'll put it someplace special when I get back to the North Pole. And," he goes on, "I'll think of you every time I look at it."

"Thank you," I say. Then, "Santa, could I ask you some questions?"

"Of course."

Now is my chance. I draw in a deep breath. "My sister and I have had lots of talks," I begin. "Well, they're really more like arguments sometimes. And, I hope this doesn't offend you, but you should know that Evvie doesn't believe in you. She doesn't believe in magic at all." Santa nods his head. "Evvie says that if there really is a Santa, he should give lots and lots of gifts to poor children, but that poor children sometimes don't get any presents at all. I said that's because you try to do other things for their families, like find houses for them to live in, or find jobs for the grown-ups. Is that right?"

"I do my best," replies Santa.

"I thought so," I say. "I bet you just sprinkle your magic around — like that sparkly misty stuff I saw when you came down our chimney." Santa smiles. "So is it true? You do something for everyone, but you do different things for different people? Like for us, you just leave a couple of presents, because we already have so much. And you give magic to other people."

"Yes, that's so," agrees Santa.

"I guess magic explains a lot of things," I go on, thinking of my conversations with Evvie. "It explains how you can fly around the entire world in just one night."

"And how I can fit everything for everyone into one pack," adds Santa, pointing to his stuffed sack.

"The elves must be magic too," I say.

"Yes. And children's letters are sent to me by magic."

"Oh. I wondered about that. Because we have always mailed letters to you by sending them up our chimney. Dad says they travel to the North Pole on a gust of wind that way. But Sarah used to address her letters to Santa Claus at the North Pole and mail them in the box in town. And *her* father said they would reach you *that* way. I guess any way works if there's magic behind it."

"Exactly so," says Santa.

Sadie, who is now sitting on the floor between Santa and me, has been following our conversation by looking back and forth from one to the other of us. She hasn't said a word, but suddenly I have the feeling that she knows the question I am about to ask and also knows that it may not have an easy answer.

"Santa," I say, and glance down at Sadie, "I have a really important question to ask you. Actually, it's more of a favor."

"All right," replies Santa Claus.

"Well..." I find that I don't quite know how to begin. "Well, my friend Sarah..."

"Yes?"

"Have you been to her house yet tonight?"

"No, not yet."

"Do you know that her father is sick?" I ask.

"Yes."

"He's *very* sick," I add. "And — Sarah probably didn't even write you a letter this year. But I know that what she wants more than anything is for her father to get well. He did come home for Christmas, but he isn't well at all. So I was wondering... could you make him well? Could you do that for Sarah? She doesn't want any presents or anything else. Just for her father to get well. When you go to her house, you don't even need to slide down her chimney. You can just throw that sparkly stuff on her roof to make her father well, and then you can keep on going."

There is a long pause during which no one says anything. Sadie stands up, though, opens her mouth as if to speak to me, then closes it again. And Santa begins pulling at his mustache.

"Tess —" he says finally.

"You don't even have to make him well right away," I interrupt him. "It can happen gradually."

"Tess —"

"Like by springtime or even summer. It would be really nice, though, if he were well for Christmas next year."

"Tess, you must understand something," says Santa, as Sadie quietly moves beside me and leans against my leg again. "I give many gifts, but I can't do everything. I do my best, but I can't find a home for every person without one, or a job for every person who needs one."

"I know that," I reply. "And I know that some people wish for gifts that don't make sense. But Sarah's father —"

"And I can't make everyone well either," continues Santa. "Do you understand, Tess?"

I look down at Evvie's boots. "Maybe," I say. "I guess so. But Santa, couldn't you please try to make Mr. Benjamin well? *Please?* Just *try?*"

Santa looks at me with kind eyes. "Tess," he says, "you have found hope, and that's a wonderful and powerful thing. Hold on to it. And if you can pass the hope on to Sarah this year, it will be the best gift you can give your friend."

Santa hasn't answered my question — at least I don't think he has — but he is pulling at his mustache again, and I realize that magic or no magic, he probably needs to be on his way.

"I guess you have to go back up the chimney now, don't you?" I say.

"I think it is time, yes," replies Santa.

I look at him, at his splendid red and white and green suit, at his kind eyes, at the faint mist that surrounds him. For a moment I forget about wishes and requests and presents and what Santa can and can't do and think simply, *I have seen the magic*. It is Christmas Eve and I am standing in our living room talking to Santa. I have *met Santa Claus*.

Santa is standing by the fireplace again, and now he lays his finger beside his nose.

Before he can nod his head, I exclaim, "Thank you, Santa! Thank you for all the presents and for talking to me. Thank you for everything."

"You're welcome, Tess. And thank you for your gift."

In a flash, Santa gives a nod, and he and his pack disappear up the chimney, leaving behind a trail of the sparkling mist.

My heart is pounding. I have met Santa. I have talked to him. I have seen his sleigh and the reindeer and the magic. But I still have questions.

"Sadie?" I say, and she turns to me. "Next year you should keep track of things you want to talk about with me on Christmas Eve, okay?"

"Okay," replies Sadie.

"Of course, *I'll* be able to talk to *you* all year long."

"That's right."

I am about to ask Sadie a question about Santa Claus, when something occurs to me. In the last few moments, Sadie has not actually spoken to me. I have heard her voice in my head, but she hasn't spoken aloud.

"Sadie?" I say.

"Yes?" she replies.

Her mouth doesn't move.

Our living room is as silent as a snowfall.

Eleven

"*Sadie?*" *I try again.*

Sadie cocks her head and looks charmingly at me, the way she does many, many times every day. But I don't hear her voice. Not aloud and not in my head.

"What happened to your voice?" I ask. "Why don't you talk to me?"

Sadie's mouth parts in a grin. She lets her tongue hang out, and she gives me her squinty-eyed look.

"Sadie . . . *Sadie*?"

Now Sadie can't seem to talk to me at all, and I don't know why. I have about a million more questions to ask her. I try to send them directly into her head, the way she sent her words into mine. I concentrate as hard as I can. *Sadie, does the magic happen like this every year?* I squeeze my eyes shut tight and imagine the words floating through the air between our heads and entering Sadie's brain. If they reach her, she shows no sign. I try speaking the words aloud. Nothing. Sadie still sits on the floor, grinning and giving me squinty eyes.

I look around the living room.

The fire has died and become glowing embers once again. Santa's snack is now minus one snowman cookie. And a few drops of hot chocolate are drying from a bit he spilled when he sipped from the mug. I peek into our stockings. There are the gifts Santa slipped into them — the kaleidoscope, the book, the puzzle, the jacks. Under the tree are the larger gifts he added. They blend in with the others so well that at first I can't locate them, but there they are — the gifts labeled "From Santa" that, in our excitement tomorrow, Mom and Dad and Evvie will each think someone else placed under the tree.

But I'll know who they're from.

I spy a corner of tissue paper on the rug and stoop to pick it up. It's all that remains of my gift to Santa. The snow globe is now riding around the world in the back of the most glorious sleigh I can imagine.

I sigh. I feel somehow both happy and cheated. I am awed by what I have seen tonight, but I can't believe that Sadie stopped talking to me just when I had so many, many questions for her. And now I won't be able to speak to her again for a full year.

But, I remind myself, Sadie can understand me. All year long when I talk to her, even if she is looking at me with her goofy grin or her silly squinty eyes, I must remember that she understands me, truly understands me, which makes for half a conversation. And half a conversation is a lot better than no conversation at all. Plus, next Christmas Eve I will be able to talk with her again.

Also, I think, as I look around the living room, making sure it's the way Mom and Dad left it when they went upstairs to bed, by next Christmas Eve Sarah's father will probably be well. Santa didn't make any promises, but I know he'll do his best.

I climb the stairs, Sadie at my side, and imagine Santa sprinkling his magic over the Benjamins' house as he and the reindeer fly by.

Christmas Day is as exciting as ever, but Sadie and I yawn our way through it since we were up so late visiting with Santa. This is the first Christmas I haven't wakened everybody at five-thirty. Mom thinks it's because I'm growing up.

"No more stumbling out of bed at the crack of dawn," she says to Dad.

It's nine o'clock before we're sitting around the living room with our stockings in our laps. I pay close attention to Mom and Dad and Evvie as they find the gifts from Santa.

When Dad reaches into his stocking and pulls out the tiny book, he looks at it and smiles fondly at Mom, who is peeling the foil off of a piece of chocolate and doesn't notice him or the book.

"Christmas morning," says Mom with a satisfied smile. "The one time it's okay to have chocolate for breakfast."

When Evvie finds the kaleidoscope she says, "Cool!" and goes on to the next gift while Dad jumps up to answer the telephone and Mom pokes at the fire.

When Mom pulls out the puzzle she says, "My, a real brainteaser," but Dad is still on the phone, and Evvie is now peering at the gifts under the tree.

"Hey," says Evvie suddenly, standing up and noticing the table on which we left Santa's snack. "What do you know. Look at that."

"Laura!" Dad calls to Mom. "It's your sister on the phone." Mom joins Dad in the kitchen.

Evvie considers the remains of Santa's snack. "Only one cookie gone," she says. "I guess Mom and Dad were pretty full from dinner. The drips of hot chocolate are a nice touch, though, aren't they?"

I glance at Sadie and see that she is regarding me solemnly. I am absolutely sure she knows what I'm thinking right now.

After breakfast, we open the presents under the tree. We are having so much fun (I jump up and down when I get a pair of roller skates with their very own key, and Evvie actually shrieks when she opens a set of curlers exactly like Maggie's) that I almost forget to watch what happens when I open the game of Monopoly and Evvie opens the box of watercolors. But I do remember in time, and I watch my parents' faces. I see their eyes twinkle as they exchange small smiles. Dad is probably thinking what a thoughtful shopper Mom is, and Mom is probably wondering when Dad secretly went to the toy store.

By lunchtime the gifts have all been opened, and

Evvie and I lie on the floor amid bits of wrapping paper and talk about our gifts. Usually Sarah and her parents come for a visit on Christmas afternoon, but not this year. Mr. Benjamin isn't allowed to leave the house, and anyway, Sarah and her mom and dad just want to spend one more day together before Mr. Benjamin returns to the hospital. I miss Sarah, but Evvie kindly shows me how to use her curlers.

That night I go to bed early (by now Mom is beginning to think I'm coming down with a cold), and Sadie crawls under the covers with me. "I'm glad you're part of the magic," I tell her. "And I can't wait until next Christmas Eve. But I'm going to talk to you all year long. You are the best, best dog." I kiss her on the top of her head, and she nestles against my side.

* * *

By New Year's Eve, Mr. Benjamin has been back in the hospital for five days. Sarah comes to our house to spend the night. Since Maggie is spending the night too, we should feel as though we're having a pajama party, but Sarah knows she's here because her mother is planning to stay at the hospital later than usual.

"She wants to be with Dad on the very first moment of this year," Sarah tells me. She pauses. "I don't think they're going to be together for the last moment of it."

I am shocked when I realize what Sarah is saying, and I don't know how to answer her. I want to tell her that I have important information, but I can't — not without also telling her what happened on Christmas Eve, which she will never believe.

New Year's Eve seems very, very long, but we try to be merry. Evvie and Maggie make confetti with us. We spend more than an hour snipping away at pieces of colored construction paper. Mom has bought several rolls of crepe paper, and we hang streamers from the living room ceiling. We play games and keep our eyes on the clock. A few minutes before midnight Mom sets out six fancy glasses. She pours champagne for her and Dad, and ginger ale for Evvie and Maggie and Sarah and me. When the clock strikes twelve, we all scream and throw the confetti in the air and shout, "Happy new year!" And I look at Sadie and think about what happened at midnight a week earlier.

Vacation ends and school begins again. Our decorations have been tucked carefully into their boxes, the boxes stowed in the attic. Dad has tossed our tree into the backyard behind the shed, where I know I will come across it during the summer, brittle and dry. In town, the lights and ribbons and garlands have disappeared, and in Mr. Vinsel's store window is a display of model trains, which is interesting but not festive.

I make a chart — my very own calendar — of the days remaining until next Christmas, until the time I can talk to Sadie and see Santa and feel the magic again.

But the holidays seem miles and miles away.

Twelve

January drags along with no interesting holidays, but we do get two snow days in a row, on a Thursday and a Friday, so we have a small unexpected vacation in the middle of the month. Then come February and Groundhog Day, and I make Sadie stand in our front yard to see if she casts a shadow, which she does, but Evvie and I can't agree on what that means.

On the day after Groundhog Day, I get busy making my valentines. I make cards for everyone in my class, for Miss Sullivan, for Evvie, for Mom and Dad and my grandparents, and for Sadie. In school we make valentine pouches out of construction paper. We tape them to our desks and watch them fill up with the cards we deliver to each other.

Miss Sullivan plans a party for our class to be held on Friday afternoon, which is actually the day before Valentine's Day. Our parents are invited, and we spend some time cleaning our classroom for them and putting our best work on the bulletin boards. Also, we memorize two poems to recite for them — "Wynken, Blynken, and Nod" and "The Owl and the Pussy-Cat." Our class will recite the poems together, except for a few solo parts, and this is called choral speaking.

By Friday morning I am beside myself with excitement. I cannot wait for the party. After recess, my classmates and I will finally be allowed to open the valentines in our pouches. Then our parents will arrive and we will have the choral speaking, followed by refreshments — punch, candy hearts, and pink cupcakes.

I am standing in our kitchen after breakfast, telling Mom about the cupcakes, surrounded by the mountain of clothing I have to put on in order to walk through the snow to the bus stop, when the phone rings. It's Sarah.

"I'm not coming to school today," she tells me.

"Are you sick?" I ask.

She sighs. "I just want to spend the day with Dad."

"Did he come home?"

"No. He's still in the hospital. But I'm allowed to visit him in his room now."

"Why don't you visit him tomorrow?" I suggest. "You're going to miss the party today."

"I know. And I'm sorry. Someone else will have to say my part in 'Wynken, Blynken, and Nod.' I want to be with Dad."

"Okay," I say. "I'll tell Miss Sullivan to keep your

valentines for you. Unless you want me to bring them home."

"That's okay," says Sarah. "You can leave them at school. I don't think I'll see you this weekend."

The Valentine's Day party is fun, but not as much fun as it would be if Sarah were there. But she isn't there, and she's right: I don't see her over the weekend. She misses a lot of school during the next couple of weeks, and then one day while we're eating lunch in the cafeteria, she tells me that her father is coming home from the hospital for the last time.

"Home for good!" I exclaim. I am absolutely thrilled. I remember my conversation with Santa Claus. I picture him sailing over the Benjamins' house in his sleigh, the trail of sparkling mist settling over their roof, seeping into the walls and rooms and sleeping people.

But Sarah isn't smiling.

And soon she stops coming to school. She stops coming over to our house too. Ordinarily, I would ask Mom and Dad about this, but now I'm afraid.

Something is happening that I don't want to know about. I try imagining Santa's magic. I imagine it as stronger and more powerful than ever. At night I sit up in bed, look out my window, remember Christmas Eve, and think that somehow everything will be set right. Somehow Santa will keep his promise to me. Sarah wanted only one gift. Surely he granted it to her. She isn't greedy. And Santa is kind and thoughtful.

But one night in the middle of March, when I haven't seen Sarah for nearly two weeks, Mom and Dad call Evvie and me into the living room and tell us to sit down. Mom's eyes are red, and Dad's face is grim. I am already in my bathrobe and I twist the belt around in my hands. Then I pull Sadie into my lap and hold her close.

Before Mom or Dad can speak, Evvie says, "It's Mr. Benjamin, isn't it?"

"Yes," says Dad.

I hold Sadie tighter.

"Did he die?" asks Evvie.

"Yes," says Dad again.

And for just a moment the only thing I can think about is Christmas Eve and standing here in the living room talking with Santa Claus. I asked him about his magic, about finding houses and jobs and making sick people well. Now I try to remember *exactly* what he said to me. He said he could do those things instead of leaving presents. Didn't he?

He said he does his best.

My lip trembles, and I feel tears spilling down my cheeks. They drip onto Sadie's back. "I don't understand. Why did he leave the hospital?" I brush at the tears, and Mom hands me a tissue.

"Because the doctors couldn't help him anymore," says Dad. "And he wanted to be at home with his family."

"When is the funeral?" asks Evvie.

"Thursday morning," Mom replies.

"Will we all go?"

"Dad and I will. I think you girls will go to school as usual."

Evvie and I have never been to a funeral. Mom and Dad always say we are too young.

"Sarah will be at the funeral," points out Evvie.

"And she'll need me," I add.

"We'll think about it," Dad says.

In the end, Evvie and I are allowed to go to the funeral. The night before, Mom looks through my closet with me. She says I must wear black to the service. The only black dress I own is the velvet one Nana Florence made. The last time I wore it was on Christmas Eve.

On Thursday morning Evvie and I eat breakfast in our nightgowns. Then we dress for the funeral. I look at my family as we leave our house. Mom and Evvie and I are in black dresses. Dad is wearing a black suit and a black-and-blue necktie. He looks grim again, and I begin to feel nervous. I do not know what to expect this morning.

"Will we see Mr. Benjamin at the funeral?" I ask as we settle into our car. I have never seen a dead person before.

"No," says Mom. "The casket will be closed." She turns around to look at me in the backseat. "Are you sure you want to go to the funeral, Tess? We could drop you off at school on the way to the church."

I actually am not sure I want to go to the funeral. But I have told Sarah I will be there and I cannot let her down.

In town we park in the lot behind our church, just as we do every Sunday. The lot is crowded. We climb out of our car and walk around to the front of the church. An usher is waiting at the door, and Dad speaks quietly to him. Then the usher leads us down the aisle to the second row of pews. We will be sitting behind Mrs. Benjamin and Sarah and Sarah's grandparents.

Some very nice music is being played on the organ, but I don't pay much attention to it. I sit and stare at my hands until Evvie nudges me and I see that Sarah and her mother are being led into the church. When they sit down, Sarah directly in front of me, I lean forward and tap her shoulder. Sarah turns around and gives me a tiny wave. She's crying. So is Mrs. Benjamin. I slide back in my seat and start to cry too. I see that Dad has slipped his arm around Mom's shoulders, and that Mom is holding Evvie's hand. Evvie reaches for mine.

I hardly hear a word the minister says during the service. I am thinking about Sarah and her father, and about Christmas and wishes and believing, and about the one thing, the *one thing*, I asked Santa for. It wasn't even my wish. It was Sarah's. And it wasn't granted.

I lift my head as the minister is saying, "... will always be remembered," and see Sarah's shoulders shaking.

This must be the saddest day of her life.

Thirteen

After the funeral, time seems to move slowly. Each day crawls by.

Sarah comes back to school, and everyone is very nice to her. The girls offer her erasers and gum. The boys choose her for dodgeball teams, and in class they never pull her chair out from under her. But something unexpected happens. Sarah and I begin to have trouble talking to each other. Maybe it's my imagination, but Sarah seems grown-up now. Being with her is like being with Mom and Dad, who can vote and drive. Since I have never done these things, I feel separate from them, and also like a little kid. And that's how I feel with Sarah.

Sarah has become very serious. She doesn't laugh, and she gets mad at me when I haven't done anything at all. One day I say to her, "Why don't you come over this afternoon? You haven't been to our house for so long. In December you came over all the time."

Sarah glares at me. "Dad was in the hospital then. Remember?"

Well, of course I remember.

I try again. "We can make doll clothes," I suggest.

"That's for babies," says Sarah.

In April we have a week off from school, which means nine days of vacation, including the weekends. Mom and Dad decide to take a trip to Florida. "We'll ask Sarah and her mother to come with us," says Mom.

I groan. "Can't we just go by ourselves?"

Mom looks at me over her glasses, and I don't say anything else.

We stay in a big old hotel on the beach, and Evvie and I are given our own room. It connects to Mom and Dad's room by a door that is usually left open, but Evvie and I are still thrilled. We pretend we are French sisters on vacation by ourselves.

Sarah and her mother are staying in a room across the hall.

On our first morning in Florida, after an evening during which Sarah and I barely speak, Mom says, "Tess, have you and Sarah had a fight?"

"No," I say, which is the truth.

I put on my bathing suit and my terry-cloth robe, and Evvie and I take towels and books outside to the beach. I spread my towel on the sand, sit down, turn my face to the sun, and realize that this is the first warm air I've felt since September.

"I'll be right back," I say to Evvie.

I run inside, knock on Sarah's door, and call, "Sarah, Sarah, you have to come outside right now! The sun is out, the sand is hot, and there are shells everywhere!"

"Really?" says Sarah.

That morning Sarah and I walk up and down the beach, putting shells into a plastic bucket. Sarah says she is going to make a collection for her father. I'm not sure what she means by this and I decide not to ask her.

All that week Sarah and I play on the beach. We go swimming. We eat fried clams. We make up plays with Evvie and put them on for our parents. On our last day in Florida, Evvie tells Sarah a joke that makes her laugh so hard she falls over in the sand. Then she begins to cry. Then she laughs again.

When the vacation ends and we return to Hopewell, Sarah and I start spending the afternoons together like we used to do. One day Sarah shows me a large cardboard carton that she has placed in the corner of her bedroom.

"Look inside," she says. "This is the collection for my father. I'm filling this box with things he would have liked."

I lift a flap. I see a painting of a tree that Sarah made in art class, a white marble, a blue jay's feather, a stone that looks like a cat's ear, and all the shells she found in Florida. I move the painting to one side and find a red-and-green macaroni chain, the chain Sarah made at my house on the day I had the first sign that I would see Santa Claus.

I lift the chain out.

"Remember when we made all those decorations?" asks Sarah.

I nod. I can barely think about Christmas now, and I haven't looked at my special calendar in weeks. I had planned to cross every day off of it until Christmas. The last day I crossed off was February 23rd.

I drop the chain back into the box, but Sarah lifts it

out again and looks at it with a small smile before placing it carefully by the painting.

In May our class starts to plan an end-of-the-year program for our parents. Miss Sullivan says that everyone has to participate in the program. We can perform alone or in groups. I do not want to perform at all, but performing with someone else is better than performing by myself, so I ask Sarah if she wants to do choral speaking with me. But Sarah says she wants to recite "Stopping by Woods on a Snowy Evening" by Robert Frost, which was her father's favorite poem. And that she wants to do it alone.

I am disappointed, but I remember Sarah's collection and understand that this is something she must do for her father. I decide to work with three other kids who have written a skit about a family who gets a pet cat. They want me to be the cat, which is fine because I won't have to say any lines.

On the morning of the last day of school, Sarah

cries and tells me that this is the first time only her mother will be able to see her in a program. I don't know what to say to Sarah. It's true. This *is* the first time. There will be lots of other times, lots of things her father will miss. This is a sad day, and I wish it could be different. Finally I say that to Sarah: "I know. It's really sad. I wish things could be different."

Sarah sniffles, then smiles at me. "I feel kind of like my father is with me, though. And he's going to hear the poem this afternoon."

At the end of the day, when it's Sarah's turn to perform, she stands up in front of our class and our parents, and says, "I'm going to recite 'Stopping by Woods on a Snowy Evening,' by Robert Frost. This was my father's favorite poem, and I'm dedicating it to him." Then she says the whole poem without even a sniffle, and at the end she smiles at her mother.

Summer comes, and as if to make up for our extra-cold and snowy winter, it is the hottest summer I can remember. Dad puts fans in the kitchen and all our bedrooms. He even puts one in the dining room, although to escape the heat, we eat most of our meals on the screened porch. Sarah's mother gets a part-time job, so Sarah spends lots of time at our house.

One lazy day when Sarah and I are so hot we can think of nothing to do except lie in the grass and watch the clouds, Sarah says to me, "You know what I can't wait for?"

"Your birthday?" I ask. Sarah's birthday is in August, and every year her mother says she can have whatever she wants for her birthday dinner, and Sarah always chooses chocolate cake and a lobster.

"Nope," replies Sarah. "Christmas."

I sit up and look at her. "Really? Christmas? But this . . ." I am trying to think of a tactful way to mention that this will be Sarah's first Christmas without her father.

"I know," says Sarah. "Dad won't be here. But I still like thinking about getting a tree, and our house when it smells like gingerbread, and having secrets from Mom. I already decided what I'm going to make for her this year."

"What?" I ask.

"A photo album, with pictures of us and Dad in it. There are all these photos in a box that Mom keeps meaning to put into an album, but she never gets around to it. So I'm going to make one for her. I'll color a cover for it and maybe decorate the pages, and write captions for all the pictures. She'll probably cry when I give it to her, but that will be okay."

I lie down in the grass again and think about trees and decorations and our church on Christmas Eve and snowy walks with Sadie. I decide that before I go to bed I will find my Christmas calendar and start crossing off the days again.

Fourteen

Summer vacation ends, and in September Sarah and I start fourth grade together in Mrs. Thompson's class. Evvie begins seventh grade at Hopewell Junior High. She says she's nervous about going off to the bigger school with the older kids, but as she boards her bus on the first day, she doesn't look nervous at all.

The warm weather lingers. Autumn is slow to arrive,

and when it does come, it isn't as chilly or as snowy as the one before. October turns to November, and I faithfully cross off each day on my Christmas calendar. One evening, after I have crossed off another box, I count the boxes remaining before December 25th. Forty-three. Forty-three days until my next chance to see Santa. I remember last year — how I felt the magic building all fall, felt it building around me, in the snow and the wind and the air.

This year is different. I think I know why. It's because I'm not the same Tess. I'm not the Tess who believes that anything can happen if you wish hard enough. I understand now that Santa can do lots of amazing things, but he can't do everything. And that sometimes he brings wonderful gifts, but they're not exactly the ones you asked for. I still believe in magic, though, and I still believe in Santa. I hope Santa knows that, knows that I still truly believe.

* * *

One day in early December Sarah comes home with me after school. The snow is flying now, flying as hard as it ever flew last year.

"Let's play outside!" says Sarah as soon as we've finished our snack.

We take Sadie into our backyard, and she bounds around in the drifts while Sarah and I flop onto our backs and make snow angels. Suddenly Sarah jumps to her feet. "I know," she says. "Let's build a snow family. Let's make one with a mother and three children and some grandparents and a dog and a cat."

"A snow dog and snow cat?" I say.

"Yes!" Sarah is grinning. She kneels down and makes a snowball. "We'll start with one of the grandfathers," she says.

We are rolling and patting and hauling and huffing and puffing when Sarah exclaims, "Can you believe there are only twenty-one days until Christmas? Just twenty-one, Tess. I can hardly wait. Mom bought wrapping paper yesterday. And I couldn't help it — I played Christmas carols on our record player last night, and wrapped up two presents. It's so exciting. You know, Mom and I are going to go to the pageant with you this year."

"Oh, goody," I reply. "We can sit next to each other and watch Evvie."

"Maybe we better not sit next to each other," says Sarah.

Evvie is going to be half of the donkey (she refuses to tell us which half), and she's not happy about it. "You and Sarah better not laugh," she has said more than once.

"Remember when Evvie was a shepherd?" asks Sarah. "And Mom and Dad and I went to church with you, and our parents shushed us for giggling when the Baby Jesus doll fell out of the manger?"

"That was when we were in first grade," I say. "And in school our class put on 'The Night Before Christmas' for the kindergartners."

Sarah grins as she plops a head onto our snow grandfather. I begin the body for a snow grandmother. I'm rolling a ball around and around the yard, and Sadie is chasing me, when I feel myself slip away. It happens so quickly that I stumble and fall on my snowball. But I don't care. I find myself thrust back into that cold starry night, the whisperings and murmurings in the air.

Love came down at Christmas . . .

I'm in that other world for just a moment, with the doves and angels and ancient songs. And then I'm back in the snowy afternoon with Sarah, who's laughing. "You squashed it!" she cries. "You squashed our grandmother!"

That night I coax Sadie into my room and sit with her on the bed for a chat. "I have something important to tell you," I say.

Sadie cocks her head and gives me her full attention.

"I understand about the Christmas magic now," I announce. I sit back and wait for a moment, forgetting that Sadie can't answer me. "At least I'm pretty sure I do." Sadie stares at me with her brown eyes. "Christmas and Santa are all about hope. Did you see how happy Sarah was this afternoon? I thought Christmas would be sad for her this year, but thinking about it makes her happy. She's looking forward to the pageant and a tree, to getting out the decorations with her mother, to shopping and baking. She's feeling hopeful again, Sadie." Sarah didn't get the gift I asked Santa to give her last year, but she found hope — Christmas magic too, I think — and that is a powerful gift.

Sadie continues to gaze into my eyes, and I'm not sure, but I believe she nods her head very slightly.

Now it is Christmas Eve and I am lying in my bed, feeling the shift in the air around me, the shift that tells me the magic is taking over.

Evvie runs into my room and jumps onto the bed, shivering because she is barefoot. We are supposed to be asleep, but Evvie is all wound up, thinking about that makeup kit. Downstairs, Mom and Dad are filling the stockings and putting presents under the tree. Evvie and I whisper together until Evvie says, "I better go back to bed. Mom and Dad will be upstairs soon."

After Evvie leaves, I look out the window at the brightening sky. Christmas is everywhere now, in that crackle in the air, among the birds settling on the roof of the Andersons' barn. Sadie slips into my room, and I grin at her. As the moon moves through the sky and the doves coo and something flutters just outside my window, I put my arm around Sadie and we sit together on the bed, sit together on Christmas Eve.

More unforgettable stories from Ann M. Martin...

Ann M. Martin
Author of the Newbery Honor Book A Corner of the Universe

A dog's life

The autobiography of

Includes AFTER WORDS™ bonus features

SCHOLASTIC

When their mother is taken away from them, stray pups Squirrel and Bone are forced to make it on their own—braving humans, busy highways, and all kinds of weather.

Ann M. Martin

A Corner of the Universe

Includes AFTER WORDS™ bonus features

SCHOLASTIC

Hattie Owen didn't think her family had secrets. Until an uncle whom she never knew about showed up—and turned her world upside down.

Newbery Honor Book

SCHOLASTIC

www.scholastic.com/annmartin

UNIDOG

A Christmas no one will ever forget...

It's Flora and Ruby's first Christmas without their parents. Luckily, they have Grandmother Min and friends Olivia and Nikki by their side. Then, Flora and Ruby's aunt pays an unexpected visit—and shakes things up in ways they never imagined.

www.scholastic.com/mainstreet

MAINST3